Pirate's Manor stood high on a cliff overlooking the sea. Great waves crashed against the rocks below, and the wind cried out like a human voice.

"It looks like a haunted house!" Sophie said. "Why do you want to go in *there*?"

"Because maybe it *is* haunted! I want to see a real ghost!" answered Matt.

"Old Stumptooth, the wicked pirate, built this house
long ago, and some say they've seen him, going from room
to room looking for something."

Sophie peered in the window. "It looks scary!"
"Let's go in!" said Matt bravely, pushing open the
old door.

Sophie followed Matt up the creaking stairs watching the shadows play tricks inside the gloomy house.

Matt got to the top step and froze. "Wh-what's that?!" A door was opening slowly. Someone or something was coming out!

"Who is it?" Sophie asked in a whisper.

"Meow!"
"It's only a cat," said Matt with a laugh.

GOLD
ENOUGH
ROOM
BLUFF
STUMPTOOTH
THE PIRATE

Matt stepped on a loose board that popped up.
"Ouch!" he said, rubbing his shin.
"What's this?" Sophie asked. Under the floor board
she saw an old piece of paper.

"It's a riddle! Listen!
    Of pirate's gold I'll say enough:
    Secret room and blindman's buff."
"What does it mean?" Matt asked. "Let's try to find
out."
    Sophie grabbed Matt's hand, and they started through
the door.
    "Hoo, hoo, HOO!" they heard and stopped still.

"It's only the wind echoing down the chimney," Sophie said, sighing with relief.

"It gives me the creeps," Matt said.

Suddenly they heard a *scritch, scritch, SCRAATCH!*

"What's that!?" yelled Sophie.

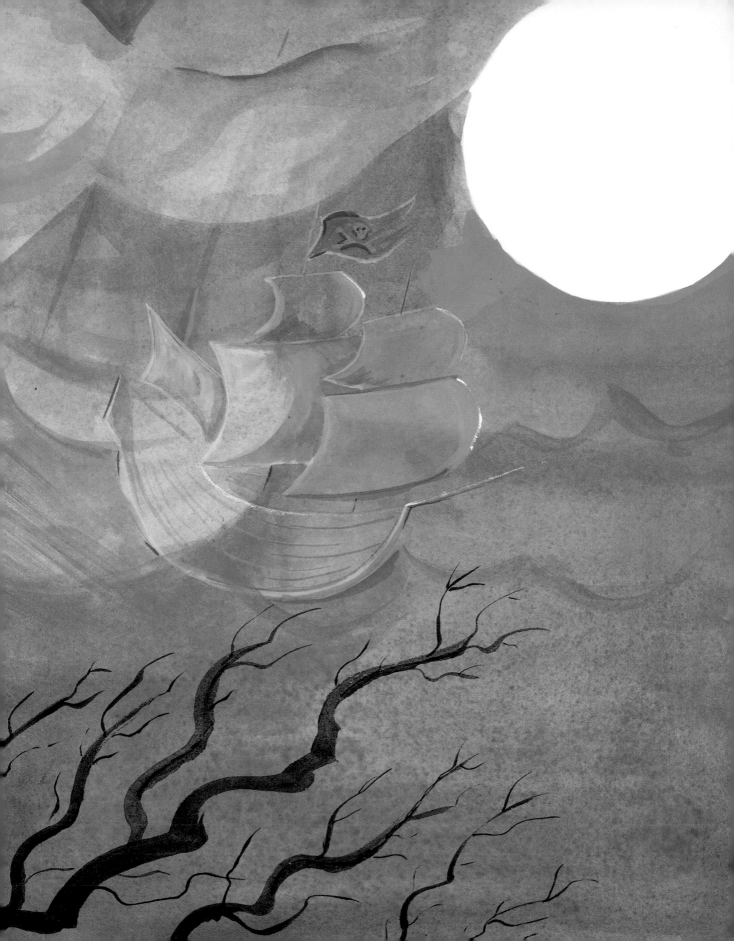

"It's only the branches scratching against the window pane," said Matt.

"Whew!" said Sophie. "Do you feel brave enough to go into that closet?" she asked.

The closet looked enormous and very spooky. Shadows danced crazily across the floor as the two children held hands and walked into the darkness.

Sophie and Matt tried not to be afraid of the strange shapes on the closet shelves.

"Look!" said Sophie. In the middle of the closet, they saw a small beam of light. Sophie could feel goose bumps on her neck.

"Behind that wall! There's something there!" she said.

DRAGON LADY

Matt pushed against the wall and a hidden door opened into an old-fashioned study with a rolltop desk, a beautiful painting of Stumptooth's famous pirate ship, Dragon Lady, and . . .

"It's STUMPTOOTH'S GHOST!" Sophie screamed. "He's coming after us!"

"No, it's just his clothes hanging up," Matt said, trying on Stumptooth's hat, "This is the secret room, all right! Now, what do we look for?"

"I know!" said Sophie. "Let's play blindman's buff as it says in the riddle and maybe we'll find out. You spin me around."

Matt took Sophie's scarf and tied it over her eyes
and spun her around. Sophie stretched out her arms
and walked straight into the picture on the wall.

The heavy painting of the pirate's ship swung open like a door!

"It's Stumptooth's treasure chest!" Sophie cried, as they lifted the heavy chest out of the wall safe.

Together, they pried open the rusty lock and threw back the lid. Doubloons and precious stones spilled out!

"Let's see what else is in this chest," Matt said.

Sophie lifted out a golden crown and put it on her head. "It's so beautiful, it must have belonged to a princess!"

"This old place could be a museum!" Matt said.

And that's what it is today.